Brown-Ears

Brown-Ears is a floppy rabbit with droopy
ears, dangly legs and a round bobbly head.
He is soft and cuddly – and Ross never goes
anywhere without him. But he has one very
bad habit – he keeps getting lost... And so
begins his great adventure.

This delightful story will comfort and
bring a smile to anyone who, like Ross, has
lost a favourite friend. It is recommended
for reading aloud to listeners from 4 years,
and for reading alone from ages 7 or 8.

Stephen Lawhead is the author of nine books
for children, including *Brown-Ears at Sea*
(a sequel to *Brown-Ears*), as well as many
best-selling fantasy novels for adults. He
lives with his family in Oxford.

BROWN-EARS

The adventures
of a lost-and-found rabbit

STEPHEN LAWHEAD

Illustrated by
ROBERT GEARY

LION
Children's Books

The author asserts the moral right to be
identified as the author of this work

Published by
Lion Publishing plc
Mayfield House, 256 Banbury Road,
Oxford OX2 7DH, England
www.lion-publishing.co.uk
ISBN 0 7459 4776 X

First edition 1989
This edition 2002
10 9 8 7 6 5 4 3 2 1 0

A catalogue record for this book is available
from the British Library

Printed and bound in Great Britain
by Cox & Wyman, Reading

Contents

1

The Best of Times

Once there was a little yellow-haired boy named Ross, who travelled the world with his parents. Wherever they went, Ross always took his favourite friend: a brown bunny, called ... well, Bunny. Bun, for short; Bunny Rabbit, for long.

Bunny was a floppy sort of rabbit with droopy ears and dangly legs, and a round bobbly head (because it wasn't sewn on very tight).

He was soft and cuddly, too, because he was made of brown fuzzy cloth – the kind little boys like to snuggle up to at night. He had brown eyes, and a yellow nose, and big blue bloomers that he wore.

And since Ross never went anywhere without Bunny, the two of them had seen and done a lot of truly amazing things.

They had flown in aeroplanes together, and ridden in trains, and buses, and cars of all kinds, and, once or twice, even a boat. So Bunny, like his friend Ross, was a pretty good traveller all in all.

But it happened that Bunny had one very bad habit: he would get lost.

Now, it maybe wasn't always his fault. Maybe he was just unlucky. Maybe it happened when he was trying his very best *not* to get lost. None of that mattered somehow; he got lost anyway.

Some people said he should have been more careful, that he should have had his head sewn on tighter, or worn a compass on his nose. Or perhaps he should have had a map sewn on his tummy so that when he *did* get lost — as he always did — he could at least find his way home again.

Still, however it was, however he tried, it couldn't be helped.

Bunny got lost and that was that.

Nothing he did made the slightest bit of difference. He would fall asleep watching television, and wake up behind the sofa. He would be playing happily by himself and the next thing he knew, he was under the bed. Once, he even found himself in the bath (or, was it the toilet? I forget). Don't ask how *that* happened.

Twice, while he was snoozing happy as you please and minding his own business, Bunny got tossed into the washing-machine with Ross's dirty clothes. He got bubbles in his ears, and it took him three days to dry out.

Now, Ross tried to keep track of Bunny. He really did his best. But Ross was just a little boy and he had enough trouble just keeping track of himself: so that *Ross* didn't end up under the bed, or behind the sofa, or in the washing-machine.

And Ross's parents? Well, one knows how grown-ups are!

In a word? H-O-P-E-L-E-S-S. They were hopeless.

Like most grown-ups, they raced around yelling a lot, and not understanding most of the time. They were often confused, and easily bewildered. And even in the best of times, they were always a little foggy.

Unfortunately, whenever Bunny got lost, it was never the Best of Times.

Well, I think you get the general idea. I won't say any more, except to say that I don't know of any other little boy who could have loved Bunny more than Ross did — bad habit and all.

2

Bunny is Lost

This adventure begins at the exact moment another adventure ends. Ross had been on holiday to Greece and the isle of Crete. Every day, for two whole weeks, he swam in the hotel swimming-pool, and sunned in the warm, warm sun. He'd been snorkelling and made sand-castles and played the days away. He'd had so much fun — why, he'd even eaten an octopus!

Of course, since Bunny was a keen traveller and always went wherever Ross went, dear old Bun enjoyed the holiday, too. For a fact, he did.

But all good things must come to an end — especially holidays — and it was soon time to return to Oxford, where Ross and his family were living just then. There was the usual hurry and flurry in getting packed, and the usual trains and boats and planes getting home.

And there was a bus.

I do wish there wasn't a bus at all. But, truth to tell, it was a very nice bus and there weren't very many people on it. Well, there never *are* at that time of the night, are there?

I want you to understand that it was very late at night. Did I say *very* late? I mean, it was extremely, horribly, terribly late. Which wouldn't have been so bad by itself, I suppose, but it happened to be at the end of an awfully long, long day as well.

So, you see how it was:

Two small children (Ross's little brother Drake was there, too). And their foggy parents.

On a bus. In the middle of the night. Exhausted. Just back from holiday. Glad to be home at last. And definitely not thinking the worst.

In fact, not thinking about anything as much as climbing into a nice warm bed for a proper good-night-sleep-tight sort of snooze.

And, of course, the very worst possible thing happened: Bunny, dear old flop-eared, fuzzy, happy-go-lucky, friend-to-all, Bunny G. Rabbit, Esq. got lost.

L-O-S-T with all capital letters lost.

Totally, utterly, and irretrievably lost.

Quite lost.

How, you wonder?

Well, the principal thing about buses is that they go. Which is splendid when you wish to get somewhere, but not nearly so splendid when you don't. And Bunny certainly didn't — wish to get somewhere, that is. Nevertheless, he did. Because the principal thing about getting lost is that you find yourself somewhere you don't want to be. And that is precisely what happened to Bunny.

Buses being what *they* are, and getting lost being what *it* is, Bunny woke up the next morning under a seat on the bus. And that is when his great adventure began.

I mean, think of it! There you are, sound asleep, dreaming of acres of carrots and absolute mounds of lettuce, and all kinds of rabbitarian delights, when ... WHOOSH! BUMP! WHEE! DUMP! SLAM!

You're ears over tail in the bin. And he was.

Bunny knew what had happened, of course. "I'm lost," he said to himself. (He was fairly well used to it by now and knew exactly how it felt.) And he settled himself to wait for Ross to show up and rescue him — which is what usually happened in these situations.

Ross would turn up sooner or later, and say something like, "There you are, crazy rabbit!"

And they would both have a good laugh about it and go off together.

But sometimes it doesn't happen like that. As much as you hope, and pray, and wish it to be, it just doesn't happen. Why it doesn't happen is one of life's little mysteries, so I won't spend too much time on it here – except to say that mooning too long over life's little mysteries doesn't get you very far. It's better to say a prayer, put your chin up, and soldier on as best you can, and be a good sport if at all possible.

So, here was dear old Bun, sitting in a rubbish bin with all sorts of nasty stuff: old bus tickets, chewing gum wrappers, greasy chip papers, sticky pop cans, crumpled newspapers, and dust, and dirt, and the usual what-have-you that gets swept out of buses and dumped in the dustbin at the bus station.

"Well, so much for adventures," thought Bunny. "It was more fun getting lost in the washing-machine."

This was a Monday and, as everyone knows, Wednesday is dustbin day in Oxford. So the dustmen came early on Wednesday morning and emptied the bin at the bus station into their dustcart.

Bunny knew what had happened because he suddenly felt himself falling through space with all kinds of junk to land in a dark, nasty place which could only be described as the inside of a dust-cart, which was precisely what it was.

Well!

Again I say, Well! What a state of affairs. What a SMELL!

I don't need to tell you that Bunny did not like this one little bit. I mean, would you?

Think of it! All those gooey eggshells, damp coffee grounds, curdly milk cartons, putrid potato peelings, slimy fish bones, stale peas, orange rinds, apple cores, worn-out shoes, ragged clothes, germy old tissues, and who knows what else?

It was a mess. Did I say mess? It was worse: it was a disaster. A dreadful disaster.

Bunny found what comfort he could by sitting on a stack of old *TV Times* and thinking, "What would Ross do in a case like this?"

Well, he couldn't imagine what Ross would do, and neither can I. So, Bunny did the next best thing: he said a little prayer, and tried to think cheery thoughts – difficult as that was in the bowels of a dustcart.

When the dustcart is full up, what happens? You've guessed! It goes to the dump. And? Right again! It dumps its load.

And no matter what happens to be in the back

— slimy fishbones, or a nice cuddly brown bunny — it gets dumped. One moment Bunny was just sitting there, reading a gardening article in the 16 May *TV Times* and the next moment he was slipping, sliding, falling down the enormous slopes of a mountain of rubbish.

He tumbled and spun and rolled and rolled and landed inside a broken teapot someone had thrown away. And there he stayed.

"This," said Bun in his most exasperated voice, "is without doubt," he said, "the most terrible — yes, I think it safe to say — the most horrible," he insisted, "horrible thing that has ever happened to me," he declared, "in my entire life," he remarked. And continued, "Worse, I will venture, than the Toilet Episode, which I had completely forgotten about until just now."

It was no picnic certainly. And no piece of cake. He was in a pickle and that was the plain, unvarnished truth.

The problem is that most things, once they end up on the dump, do not come back again. Which is the whole point, really. I mean, who would throw away anything if it kept coming *back*? Suppose you tossed out your holey old socks, and presto! next day there they are back in your drawer. Or, that cold, squidgey, left-over porridge: ZIP! back in your bowl for supper.

YISH! I mean, it would not do. So, Bunny was in a fix and no mistake. The best he could hope for — if you call this hoping for something — was to find some way to help him pass the time. Because Bunny, like it or not, was going to be visiting Mount Rubbish for a very long time.

3

Big Hairy Rats

The day passed slowly. Luckily, it didn't rain, which would have made things worse. (Have *you* ever smelled *wet* rubbish?) "At least," Bunny consoled himself, "I am dry, and that is something. And I have my teapot which, although a touch on the snug side, is pleasant enough if you aren't too particular." And he wasn't.

Around about supper-time he started feeling a little sad. Not for himself, you understand, but for Ross. "How Ross must miss me," he thought unhappily. "Because, if he misses me even a fraction as much as I miss him, then it is a very great deal indeed!" And then he said a little prayer that he would find his way back to Ross very soon. It was not the first time he had prayed that prayer, nor would it be the last.

Ross did miss Bunny, of course. As much as a

little boy *could* miss anything, which is quite a lot, actually.

Well, night came. And with the darkness came rats. Did I say rats? I mean long-tailed, yellow-toothed, scaly-footed, beady-eyed rats. *Rodenticus Giganticus*, to be precise. The meanest, greasiest rats in the whole miserable rat business.

All at once, there they were, swarming over Mount Rubbish, sniffing here and there with their pointy snouts, prying into everything with their long, ratty fingers. Bunny watched them, afraid. He had never seen rats so big and ugly.

One meaty rat saw Bunny and scrabbled over to him.

Now, it is a well-known fact that this kind of rat does not like cuddly brown rabbits. These rats do not like cuddly *anything* of *any* description.

This rat sneered right in Bunny's face. "What are *you* doing here? You're not a rat." He said this as if being a rat was a singular honour and not to be wasted on lesser creatures.

"I'm a cloth rabbit, now that you mention it," replied Bunny, trying not to sound frightened.

The rat glared at Bunny with his beady eye. "You are trespassing. I suggest you leave before I eat you."

"Frankly, I would leave at once, but I seem to

be stuck in this teapot. And then there is the matter of being lost."

"Ha, ha!" laughed the rat wickedly. "You're lost! I knew it! Things are always getting lost here."

"I can quite imagine," said Bunny.

Rat licked his rat chops. "I think I'll eat you now and teach you a lesson," he said. The big rat crawled closer, his yellow teeth gleaming sharp in the moonlight.

"Help!" cried Bunny.

The rat jumped.

SNAP! The rat teeth snapped.

But Bunny was gone. Just at the instant the rat jumped, the teapot slipped and began rolling down Mount Rubbish. The rat turned and began chasing his dinner down the slope.

"W-H-O-A!" cried Bunny. He might have saved himself the trouble of shouting, for at that moment the teapot hit a brick and smashed and Bunny was tossed up, up into the air. And fell down, down on to a mouldy mattress with the springs bulging out.

And what was sitting on that stinky old mattress? You guessed it, a group of stinky old rats.

Poor old Bunny landed with a bounce and the rats took one look at him, shouted "DINNER!"

and dived in.

Bunny squirmed and closed his eyes.

But the rat teeth did not bite. In fact, he did not feel a thing. He opened his eyes and saw the rats scampering away over the rubbish dump and . . . What was that? The BIGGEST rat of all?

No.

It was a dog.

4

A Bad Situation
Made Slightly Better – Almost

The dog had seen the rats on the mattress, licking their greedy rat chops. Dogs have no love for rats, and so he said to himself, "I'd be less than a dog, if I didn't go and see what they're about." Or words to that effect.

So, he did just that. The rats saw him coming and skedaddled – because rats are natural cowards no matter how *Rodenticus Giganticus* they are.

The dog barked once, snatched up Bunny in his jaws, and trotted off.

By this time, Bunny had worked out what had happened. He was not quite certain that being snatched up by a hungry dog was a great deal better than being devoured by hungry rats. It amounted to much the same thing in the end.

Either way, he didn't seem to have much choice in the matter. As the dog held him securely in his jaws, there was nothing to do but wait and see. After a while the dog got tired of running and sat down. He dropped Bunny on the ground in front of him. Bunny raised his head and looked around.

"I thank you for saving me from the rats, sir," he said, thinking that it never hurt to be polite.

"*Ach Du Lieber!*" said the dog (he was an Alsatian). "A talking rabbit."

"Cloth, actually," replied Bunny. "But I can speak when I want to."

"Whatever vere you doing in there?"

"I am rather lost at the moment, I'm afraid," explained Bunny in his best British manner. (Even American rabbits learn to speak this way in Great Britain and it helps immensely.) "I don't seem to know where I am. Worse yet, I don't know where I ought to be." He sighed and came to the point. "I seem to be in rather a jam. Perhaps you wouldn't mind helping me out a bit."

The dog considered this for a moment.

"I'm sure my master would reward you," Bunny added. "Bones and such. My master has ever so many bones, you know."

The dog made up his mind at once.

"You vill tell me the name of your meister, please," said the dog. "And take you to him I vill."

"Wonderful!" cheered Bunny. "By the way, my name is Bunny Rabbit."

"It iss a pleasure," said the dog. "Mine name iss Otto. Now then, your meister's name, what iss it please?"

"His name is Ross. That's r — I mean, capital R, o — small o, double s."

"Never heard of him," said the dog. "But no matter. Where does he live?"

"That's just the point. I haven't the slightest idea. I've never had to find my way home before. Ross always took care of things like that."

"Vell, paid attention you maybe should have," sniffed the dog.

"Oh, I quite agree," sighed Bunny. "But that doesn't help very much right now, I'm afraid."

"No, it certainly doesn't," agreed the dog. "I tell you what I do. To the Animal Shelter I vill take you. They vill know what to do mit you." With that Otto gently picked Bunny up in his mouth and trotted off.

Well, it would have been a fine idea, except for the bothersome fact that, it being the middle of the night, the Animal Shelter was closed. Bunny and Otto sat down on the pavement in front of the A.S. to think. And what they thought was this: that they were very tired and that it probably wouldn't hurt to curl up right where they were and go to sleep and see what the morning might bring.

5

What the Morning Brought

Bunny and the dog slept as well as they could on the pavement. Bunny had slept in all kinds of places so he was not fussy, except that he preferred Ross to be there.

Still, all in all, it was a good sleep, if a trifle short because Otto jumped up at dawn's first light and said, "It iss time to visit ze butcher! I vill return mit breakfasht!" And off he went.

Bunny didn't even have time to explain that rabbits, cloth or otherwise, did not, and certainly never would, eat anything remotely connected with a butcher's shop. In fact, rabbits stayed as far away as possible from any sort of meat shop, for fear of becoming Today's Special Offer.

But Otto had gone before Bunny could say "alfalfa".

So Bunny settled back to wait. But he didn't

wait long, for what should come whizzing by but a milk float. It stopped right in front of him and the milkman climbed out, nearly stepping on Bunny's ear.

" 'Ello, 'ello," said the milkman. "What 'ave we 'ere then? Looks like a rabbit!"

He bent down and picked up Bunny. "My little Trixie will like this'n 'ere. What luck!" With that he stuffed Bunny into the pocket of his blue uniform and went on his way.

The milkman seemed a friendly sort, as milk-people usually are. Nevertheless, Bunny was not exactly thrilled with the idea of meeting Trixie.

"I am certain that little Trixie is a very nice child," said Bunny to himself. "A remarkable child, no doubt. But Trixie isn't Ross."

It was dark and warm inside the milkman's pocket, which Bunny liked. It also smelled like the inside of a cheese shop, which he didn't like nearly so much. But, all in all, it was better than a teapot full of rats; so, with that thought, he folded his ears over his eyes and went to sleep.

He woke up just as the milkman arrived home from his day's work. "Oi! I'm 'ome, ducks!" he called as he clumped in at the door.

The milkman's wife met him with a kiss and a sorry report. " 'Ello, love. Yer little Trix is down-'earted, dear. Why don't you see if you

can cheer 'er up?"

"Well, today's 'er lucky day, then," said the milkman. "I've got the very fing in me pocket, I 'ave."

The milkman went to his daughter's door, which was shut and locked. He knocked. There was no answer.

"Trixie, it's yer Daddy, dearest. Open the door, love, I've got a present for you — a cheer-you-up sort of present."

I should explain that Bunny had seen lots of children in his life and he'd heard lots of different cries, whines, tantrums, and fits of all kinds. But he had never heard a whine that made his fur bunch up into little prickly balls.

He heard it now.

"I don't want it!" came this angry fur-bunching whine. "Go away!"

"Oh, Trixie," said her mother, "it's yer Mum. Do yerself a favour, dearie, and open up this door and see what Daddy's got fer you. You'll like it, I know."

From the other side of the door came that horrible shrieky whine again. "Is it a pony?"

"No, dearest dove, I don't fink it's a pony."

"Then . . . I DON'T WANT IT!"

"It's a rabbit, dovey," said Trixie's father. "And it's very cute, love," added her Mum.

"Why not 'ave a peek then?"

After a few moments the door opened. A fat, freckle-faced girl with a turned-up nose, frizzy red hair, and baggy black socks stood frowning right into Bunny's face.

She grabbed Bunny with a pudgy hand, took one look at him and whined, "He's not a *real* bunny!"

"But it's quite a nice one," said the milkman. "I found 'im on me rounds."

"BUT I DON'T WANT IT!" screamed darling little Trixie. And with that, she heaved Bunny across the room.

He sailed tail over ears through the air to land on a very messy shelf. And there he stayed.

6

Trixie's Den of Horrors

The door slammed shut and Bunny was left alone to survey his dismal surroundings. Did I say dismal? I mean appalling — in the strongest sense of the word. I say appalling because although Trixie's room might have been pleasant enough ordinarily, dear little Trixie was a very messy girl. She was messy enough for any ten normal children.

In fact, she was so messy she *invented* messes. She could, without any difficulty whatsoever, have got into The Messiest Child Alive category.

Anyway, what Bunny saw in Trixie's room was enough to make him pine for Mount Rubbish. It was really that bad.

There were dirty clothes everywhere, and biscuit crumbs, gravel, sweet wrappers, shoes without laces, laces without shoes, mouldy apple cores, smashed toys, melted ice creams, gungey cereal bowls, school books, broken crayons, empty tins, records without jackets, rancid fish and chip papers and elaborate heaps of rubbish of varieties, sizes, and descriptions far too numerous (not to mention disgusting) to mention.

Let's just say that Trixie's room made Mount Rubbish look like Kew Gardens.

That was what Bunny saw. And it made him a little sick in his stomach. "I think," he said bravely, "that I might prefer the rats."

He said this and then looked around quickly, lest he'd spoken too hastily and there actually *were* a few big, beefy rats lurking in the corners. Happily, there were no rats. But when it comes to snakes, spiders, bats, and beetles we can't be too certain.

As Bunny looked around him on the shelf, what he did see were a sad-faced clown and a one-eyed, one-eared bear that appeared decidedly out-of-sorts. And both of them were staring at him.

"How do you do?" asked Bunny politely. "My name is Bunny Rabbit."

"Whatever your name is," said the bear, "don't even *think* of staying here."

"Oh, Grizzle," moaned the clown, "I do wish you wouldn't be so rude. Of course, he's not staying. Are you, Mr Rabbit?"

"Well, I had not planned on staying exactly," Bunny began.

"There, you see?" said the clown. "No need to bite his head off. He's leaving." To Bunny he said, "You're leaving at once, aren't you?"

"Well, not exactly," admitted Bunny.

"When then," demanded the grumpy bear, "exactly?"

"I seem to be lost," explained Bunny.

"You are lost, all right," sighed the clown. "Quite lost. Most of us here are."

"No, I mean..." started Bunny, but the bear interrupted.

"He's a free-loader. I knew it. Lost Property written all over him. Well, it won't work here. We don't like your kind coming around poking your noses in where you're not wanted."

"I — I'm not sure I know what you mean," said Bunny.

"You want it spelled out for you?" threatened the bear.

"What Grizzle means," put in the clown, "is that we are fairly tight for space here — what with one thing and another. It wouldn't do for just anyone to come barging in easy as you please and start making a fuss. Now that you understand, I'm sure you'll do the right thing."

"I'd be happy to go home if *that's* what you mean," replied Bunny. "This isn't the friendliest place I've ever been."

"Right!" cried the bear. "That does it. Say goodbye to your nose!"

"Now Grizzle, he didn't mean it, I'm sure," the sad-faced clown sighed sadly. "Let's face it, this isn't exactly Buckingham Palace. By the way, my name is Mr Biz."

"Glad to meet you," said Bunny.

"Speak for yourself, Sad-Sack," sneered Grizzle. "I happen to like it here."

"You would," said the clown. "But look at me. I used to smile. This frown on my face used to be the biggest grin you ever saw. And Grizzle here, not only did he have *two* ears and *both* eyes, he also had a very nice blue-striped night-shirt and a big red ribbon."

"It was awful," grumbled the bear. "I like it better now."

"Oh no you don't," yelled the clown. "You're only *saying* that. Anyway, you're a bear. You don't understand the finer things of life."

"Oh, yeah? I'll bite your nose off. Is that fine enough for you?"

Bunny feared that this might go on all night,

35

so he said, "Please, I don't see how this is going to help me find my way back home to Ross at all."

"Who wants to help you?" growled the bear. "Get lost."

"But that is precisely what I *have* done," Bunny reminded him. "And here I am."

"And here you'll stay," snapped Grizzle. "So get used to it."

"I really don't think that's possible," quivered Bunny.

At that moment Trixie stormed back into the room. She shifted a few of the rubbish heaps and found an extremely rumpled nightgown which she proceeded to put on — *over* her clothes. Then, yawning like the Grand Canyon, she went to bed without even brushing her teeth!

"You see what I mean?" whispered Mr Biz. "And she leaves the lights on all night, too. It's terrible."

"I don't think I'm going to like it here." Bunny dabbed at his eye with his paw.

"Was it nice where you came from?" asked Mr Biz.

"Who cares?" sniffed Grizzle.

"Oh, it was very nice," Bunny told him. "My master was an exceptional boy. Intelligent, brave, courteous — in short, a joy to be with."

"Poo! Poo! Poo!" mumbled the bear. "Sounds like a regular Boy Scout."

"He sounds a prince," said the clown. "Not at all like Mad Madam Mim over there. Why, I could tell you stories..."

"Aw, quit your belly-aching," growled Grizzle.

"I will not!" shouted the clown. He leaned over and whispered to Bunny. "He's always like this. He's jealous because *I* came from Hamley's. They got *him* with petrol coupons."

"That's it!" shouted the bear. "Your nose is history!"

"Wait!" said Bunny. "You'll wake up Trixie."

That stopped them at last. "Now then," said Bunny, "we've got to find a way to get me out of here."

"Impossible," muttered Grizzle. "This room might as well be a black hole."

"He's right," sighed Mr Biz. "Once you're in this den of horrors, you never get out. You know, there are dirty socks down there that have never seen the light of day! We're all doomed."

"We'll see about that!" said Bunny. And he meant it.

7

The Great Escape

Time passed. A very great deal of time, actually. Months in fact. Quite a few of them.

Poor old Bunny was still trapped in Trixie's room on the shelf where she had flung him and never so much as cast her spoiled little eyes again.

And there he might have stayed with mournful Mr Biz and grumpy Grizzle if it hadn't been for a sudden and unexpected development: Trixie got the mumps.

Let's put this in perspective, and say that if what other children got was mumps, our dear little Trix got MUMPS!!

Her face swelled up like an enormous freckled balloon. Her eyes bulged. Her tongue hung out. Her nose ran. She lay on her messy bed and moaned constantly, day and night.

Trixie's mum was beside herself. Little Trixie had never had so much as a sniffle before, and now *this!* Whatever was to be done?

She took one look at Trixie and called the doctor. The doctor came with black bag in hand, took one look at Trixie, said "Mumps", and scribbled out a prescription for mumps medicine. "Give her this," said the doctor. Then, peering around the room, he turned a little green and gaggy, and whispered, "And, for heaven's sake, get this room fumigated at once!"

Trixie's mum agreed with the doctor "It could do with tidyin' up, I suppose. Never mind, I'll 'ave a go, doctor."

"You do that, or I'll have this room declared a National Health Hazard," he said grimly.

Five teams of professional cleaners attempted Trixie's room and all five were forced to retreat, beaten and disgusted.

So, in the end, Trixie's mum took it on. She assembled shovels and barrows and rakes and implements for lifting and shifting. She armed herself with pesticides, cleaners, rubber gloves, goggles, chemical-proof clothing, steel-toed shoes, and a lead-lined apron, and she took it on.

Hercules, that mythic Greek superman of fable fame, had an easier time mucking out the Aegean Stables. But Trixie's mum persevered and after the third or fourth day she began to see the floor again. On the fifth day there were actually clean patches and a pattern could be made out on the carpet. On the sixth day the sun shone through the windows.

And on the seventh day, Trixie's mum reached the shelf where Bunny sat with Grizzle and Mr Biz.

" 'Ello," Trixie's mum said, "what 'ave we got 'ere? I remember you, I do."

She picked up Bunny. "Trixie, dearest, what do you want me to do with this cute brown bunny?"

"Throw it away," moaned Trixie in a voice that sounded as if she had a mouth full of broken marbles.

"Oh, we don't like to throw it away, dear, do we? No, I shouldn't think so. 'E's a cute little bunny 'e is. And this 'ere clown and bear — why, the three of 'em are ever so cuddly-like. Don't you want 'em any more, love?"

"No!" shouted Trixie (she might have gained the mumps but she had not lost any of her endearing charm), "I hate them all! Get rid of them! I want new ones! New ones! Do you hear? I want all new ones. And I want them RIGHT NOW!!"

"Yes, lovey, I'm sure you do. I'll just take

these away then, shall I? There, that's better."

And so Trixie's mum bundled them into a bright green plastic rubbish bag with a lot of Trixie's old dresses and socks and took them away. She put the rubbish bag outside the front door and went back to cleaning Trixie's room.

"This is really super, I must say," sighed the sad-faced clown. "A one-way trip to the rubbish tip."

"It's *your* fault," growled Grizzle, nudging Bunny dangerously. "This would never have happened if *you* hadn't shown up. I hold you responsible."

This made Bunny slightly angry. "I fail to see what I had to do with Trixie's mumps," he said.

"That's right," said Mr Biz, "it's a virussy thing and all that, mumps is. Our fuzzy friend here had nothing at all to do with it."

"Well, what's he going to do about it now? That's what I want to know," snapped Grizzle.

Bunny had to admit that he did not have any plans at the moment, but added hopefully, "Look at it this way: at least we're out of Trixie's room. Anything that happens now is bound to be an improvement!"

"It had better be," grumbled the bear, "or goodbye ears!"

"Oh, I do hope whatever is going to happen

happens soon," moaned Mr Biz. "It's getting hot in this bag. Not to mention stuffy."

These mournful words were scarcely out of Mr Biz's mouth when WHOOSH! WHEE! the rubbish bag was sailing through the air. It landed with a BLUMP! a few moments later; there was a CLANK!, a RUMBLE, a ROAR! and they were off.

"You had to open your mouth," growled Grizzle. "Well, it had better be a nice rubbish tip, that's all I have to say."

It wasn't, of course. Grizzle found quite a few more things to say, and he said them. Loudly and often.

8

Out of the Bag
and into the Baggage

What had happened, if you haven't already guessed, was that Trixie's mum, having run out of her regular black rubbish bags owing to the prodigious mess of Trixie's room, had had to use green rubbish bags.

Not a big thing, you might think, and nothing to get upset about certainly. Only (and it is rather a large ONLY) the clothes cleaners which, every Thursday, like clockwork, picked up the milkman's dirty uniforms and whisked them away to be cleaned, only ever used green rubbish bags. This is how they avoided picking up the wrong bags. (This happens now and then, although Clipper Cleaners do not like to admit it as it tends to be embarrassing in a professional business climate.)

However that may be, this unadmitted mistake occurred at a most opportune moment and consequently saved Bunny's ears — at least for the time being.

The bag rolled around the streets of Oxford, Woodstock, Kidlington, Headington, and Abingdon, before finally being opened and emptied into a bin at the High Wycombe headquarters of Clipper Cleaners: *Specialist Launderers for the Smart-Looking Professional: Uniforms Our Forte*.

Once loaded, the bin was coupled to other bins and trundled along on tracks in a sort of dirty clothes train. The train moved through a regular laundry factory full of sloshing, whirring, steamy machines performing various washing functions.

Bunny had already guessed what was happening. He had some small experience with dirty laundry, you will remember. This experience was about to stand him in good stead.

"It's really not so bad," Bunny started to explain. "The bubbles are the main thing to watch out for: getting them in your ears — that sort of thing."

"What *are* you going on about?" demanded Grizzle.

"Yes, do explain," agreed Mr Biz. "I seem not

to have picked up the thread at all."

Bunny took a deep breath. "I have a strong suspicion that we are about to be washed, gentlemen. I suggest taking defensive measures."

"What sort of defensive measures would you recommend at this point?" inquired the clown. "I'm not very waterproof, I'm afraid."

"Just let them try to wash me," growled Grizzle. "I'll bite their noses off!"

"It's actually very simple, once you catch the trick. Just hold your breath and keep your hands over your eyes . . . Oh, yes, and put your thumbs in your ears. I've seen Ross do it a jillion times."

"It sounds devilishly difficult to me," whined the clown. "I don't think I'll manage it at all."

"Bears don't have thumbs," sneered Grizzle. "We don't need them."

"Suit yourselves," said Bunny.

Just then the bin they were riding in was tipped into a gigantic tumbler full of hot, sudsy water.

They were washed — which is to say they were sloshed, sudsed, pummelled, frothed, spun and cold rinsed. All in the space of about five minutes. Then they were tumbled into another bin and trundled along to the drier.

"That wasn't so bad," said Bunny.

"I'm waterlogged!" sputtered Mr Biz.

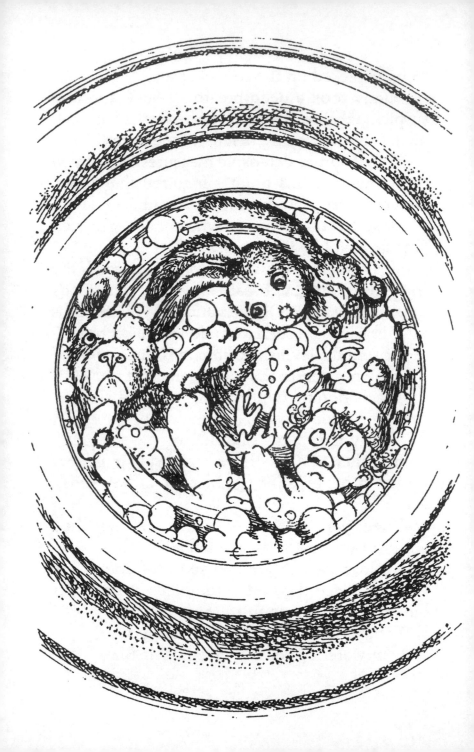

Grizzle was too wet to speak. He merely gurgled a soggy but eloquent grunt.

The drier was toasty warm, and not half dizzy-making once you fell into the circular rhythm of the thing. The three friends emerged twenty minutes later lighter, fluffier, bouncier, softer, fuller and fatter than they had been in years.

"There, you see?" said Bunny. "That's it. The worst is over."

"What happens now?" wondered the clown.

"I'm not sure," replied Bunny, reaching the end of his experience. "But I think the worst is over. I mean, I hope it is.

9

Providence

They soon found out, for the bin rolled into Sorting Room B, an enormous room where the laundry was sorted, tagged and sent along to Folding Room C where it was folded and re-bagged for delivery.

All, that is, if they had been uniforms — which obviously they weren't. So it happened that as soon as they were dumped out on to Sorting Table Sixteen, Sorter Seven noticed the mistake and pressed a red button, which summoned a Shift Supervisor.

"Yes, Sorter Seven?" asked the Shift Supervisor when she appeared. "What seems to be the problem?"

" I seem to have toys here, Shift Supervisor."

"Toys, Sorter Seven?"

"Toys, miss."

"What sort of toys?"

"Boys' toys, I should think."

"Boys' toys, Sorter Seven?"

"Boys' toys, Shift Supervisor."

"May I see them, please?"

"Right, here they are, miss." Sorter Seven scooped up the three stuffed toys and handed them to the Shift Supervisor, who took them directly to her office.

This was Standard Operating Procedure for all non-emergencies of this type: section 22 of the Launderers' Code, sub-section 35, paragraph 4. And I quote: "All non-clothing items of a wayward nature shall be held in the Shift Supervisor's office for a time not less than thirty-six hours nor exceeding forty-eight hours, after which time – assuming no attempt by a third party to claim said items – said items may be disposed of at the Shift Supervisor's discretion."

This "disposed of" had the three friends slightly worried. It might mean anything from Mount Rubbish to being shredded into tiny little bits at a recycling centre and used as non-organic insulation in the padded envelopes of Her Majesty's Postal Service.

This was worrisome all right, and no mistake. And they had two whole days to worry about it. That's plenty of time to jump to all the worst conclusions, and quite a few on the Ultimate Disaster list. (Believe it or not, there are several on the U.D. list actually *worse* than being shredded into tiny bits for postal padding.)

But sometimes what happens to you is far kinder than your worst fears because Providence is involved. Not luck, not chance or fate: Providence.

Does luck *care*? Does chance have a *heart*? Does fate want you to be *happy*?

No.

But Providence does. And even though people talk carelessly of chance and luck, it is Providence that they are really talking about. How else does one explain all the millions of good things that happen all the time whether anyone is looking or not?

Well?

10

Riding on the 7.09

After two days of sitting in a huddle on top of the Shift Supervisor's filing cabinet, the toys were stuffed into a plastic Sainsbury's shopping bag by the Supervisor who intended, no doubt, to drop them into the nearest available recycling box.

What happened, however, was quite a different thing altogether. Providence, you remember.

At any rate, the three toys soon found themselves on the luggage rack in a carriage on the *Great Malvern* heading for Paddington Station by way of Didcot and Reading.

Now, if you know anything about trains at all, you would know that this particular train was the infamous 7.09 — one of the most notorious commuter traps in all of British Rail's Greater

London Railway System. I mean to say, this train was so crowded that the guards had given up punching tickets altogether, reasoning that no one would ride on a train this crowded if they did not hold a ticket to do so. People were usually jammed into the carriages so tightly that they were forced to – GASP! – exchange greetings! Space was at such a premium that complete strangers had to – HORROR! – look at one another! And children up to the age of sixteen had to – OH MY GOSH! – sit on their parents' laps!

Luggage racks were crammed with bags, satchels, suitcases, briefcases, and all manner of backpacks – some so big that they dwarfed the people attempting to carry them.

And it was in one of these luggage racks on the jam-packed 7.09 that Bunny, Mr Biz and Grizzle found themselves. Squashed between the solid black briefcase of a well-flannelled chartered accountant from Wotton Major, and a bright green nylon zippered tote-bag belonging to a computer science student from Taiwan. It was not a pretty sight.

To make matters worse, the heating in the coach was stuck full on, and the chartered accountant refused to open the window.

"Whew!" said Mr Biz. "If the crush doesn't kill

me, this roasting will."

"Where are we going? That's what I want to know," demanded Grizzle.

"I think I heard someone say Paddington — " replied Bunny. "I've heard that word before. Now let me see ... " Bunny searched his memory for clues and, just as Grizzle was getting ready to say something nasty, he shouted, "I've got it!"

"You might as well give us the bad news," sighed the gloomy clown. "I'm getting used to it."

"But it's *good* news," Bunny told him. "Paddington Station — I knew that name rang a bell. It's a very special train station. It's the home of Paddington Bear."

"Never heard of him, either," sniffed the bear.

"He's a stuffed toy just like us, and he got lost and ended up somehow in Paddington Station with a note attached to him saying 'Please Help This Bear,' or some such thing."

"Really?" wondered the clown.

"Yes, I remember Ross's mother reading a story about it to Ross and Drake. Apparently, he's quite a famous bear — hero of sorts."

"So?" sneered Grizzle, who rather fancied himself a hero of sorts.

"Don't you see?" said Bunny. "If any train

station knows what to do with lost toys, Paddington Station does. I mean, if one *must* be a lost toy, this is the ideal place to be lost in."

"Well, I certainly hope so," replied Mr Biz. "I'm getting a little tired of bumping around in plastic bags and such. I'd rather welcome a change."

A change is just what they got.

11

Nine Million Pigeons
Can't Be Wrong

Paddington Station may very well be a splendid place for lost toys. Unfortunately, our three misplaced friends did not have the opportunity of finding out firsthand. For no sooner had the 7.09 rolled in than the commuters made a mad dash for the taxi-stand.

The Sainsbury's bag was snatched up by one of the passengers who thought it was dinner. This passenger — we'll call her Ms X — grabbed the bag and entered the chase for the taxis.

By some miracle, Ms X nabbed a cab — which she agreed to share with four other commuters. They rode into central London, getting out at various places along the way: Buckingham Palace, Harrods, Marble Arch, just to mention three. Anyway, by the time the taxi reached

Trafalgar Square, the only passengers left were, you guessed it: Bunny, Mr Biz, and grumpy old Grizzle, sitting in their Sainsbury's carrier bag under the taxi's folding seat.

"Paddington Station looks ever so similar to the inside of a London taxi," growled Grizzle. "I ought to bite your nose off."

"Go ahead," sighed Bunny. "If it will make you feel better, I'm all for it."

"Oh, leave him alone," snapped Mr Biz. "It isn't his fault, you know. I don't see you having any ideas. At least Bunny tries. He really does."

This conversation might have gone on for quite a long time, but it was cut short by the taxi driver, who noticed the bag in the back of his cab and retrieved it.

"Hello?" he said. "Someone's gone and left their shopping, they have. Pity, that. Let's have a little look then."

He poked his nose into the bag. "Stuffed toys?"

He looked again. "Well, well. What am I going to do with stuffed toys?"

Of all the things he might have done, this cabby chose perhaps the *worst* thing possible — from a stuffed toy's point of view, that is. He took the bag and placed it smack between the paws of one of the lions on Nelson's Column,

right in the middle of Trafalgar Square.

"Someone's going to have a giggle opening that bag," he chuckled as he walked away. Not so much a giggle as a squawk, as it turned out. Because the moment the cabby turned away thirty-seven pigeons descended on the bag and began pecking away.

It is a well-known fact that pigeons are probably the most curious of all birds. They are certainly the peskiest. And since there are nine million pigeons in Trafalgar Square, not much goes on there that does not catch their attention.

"Now what?" sighed Bunny, mostly to himself. "I had hoped for something better than being pecked to bits by a flock of pesky pigeons. I'll *never* get home to Ross at this rate."

"It could be a lot worse, I suppose," pipped Mr Biz, trying to sound more hopeful than he felt. "I mean, nine million pigeons can't be wrong... can they?"

"Still," he added wistfully, "I wish they wouldn't peck at our bag so. It's giving me a headache."

"If they don't stop," growled Grizzle bear, "I'll bite their beaks off!"

Bunny said nothing. He was thinking. And what he was thinking was none too cheerful. It was one thing to spend a pleasant afternoon with the pigeons at Trafalgar Square; it was quite another to spend a chilly night there. You see, he'd heard all about the sort of people you might meet in a big city like London — people who shaved their heads and dyed their skin (and vice versa), and ... well, it didn't bear thinking about.

Actually, pigeons and punk-rockers were not the worst things lurking about. As bad as they may be, there are still worse things sneaking around the city. And, wouldn't you know it, one of them came along just at that moment: a coachload of tourists. And all of them armed to the teeth with Nikon cameras and Sony Walkmen and Panasonic videotape recorders and who knows what else.

The coach rolled to a stop and the tourists poured out. One of them walked over to Nelson's Column aiming his camera lens. And, in the view-finder, he found a view of a Sainsbury's carrier bag.

A plastic shopping bag is not usually considered extremely photogenic. But, like Mount Everest, it was there; so the tourist took a picture of it — pigeons and all. And then he walked over to see what was inside the bag that the pigeons had been so interested in.

Just as he reached for the plastic handles he

remembered something he'd been seeing on signs and hearing over loudspeakers ever since landing at Heathrow:

DO NOT LEAVE BAGS UNATTENDED!

And:

REPORT ALL SUSPICIOUS
LUGGAGE TO THE POLICE AT ONCE!

Well, here it was: as suspicious a bit of baggage as he'd ever seen. And totally unattended. Yes, indeed. So, he did what any right-thinking tourist would do. He ran to find the nearest bobby.

"Pardon me," he said, "this luggage is unattended, please. I report it to you, thank you very much."

The bobby took one look at the bag, bulging dangerously there between the paws of one of Nelson's lions. "Right!" he said, and began blowing his tin whistle for all he was worth as he raced for the nearest police box.

12

Bombs Away!

Less than three minutes later a van came flying up, all four tyres squealing on the pavement. Men with loudspeakers jumped out and began yelling, "Get back! Get back! Evacuate the area immediately!"

"Oh, oh," said Bunny, "something's happening. I wonder what it is." And he put his eye up to a pigeon-pecked hole and peeped out.

"What is it?" whispered Mr Biz. "What do you see? What's happening out there? Why has it gone so quiet?"

What Bunny saw was this: a blue van with big white letters on its side that spelled out B-O-M-B and S-Q-U-A-D.

"Gosh!" said Bunny. "The Bomb Squad is here."

"The Bomb Squad? But that means..."

shuddered Mr Biz, "there must be a bomb somewhere."

Bunny continued, "What's more, the bomb disposal men appear to be coming this way."

"Oh, dear!" cried the clown.

"What else do you see?" asked Grizzle.

"They've got this long pole and a lead box and they're reaching *for us!*"

The next thing they knew they were being grappled by a hook on the end of a pole and the Sainsbury's bag was whizzing through the air.

"Here we go again!" grumbled the grumpy bear. "Just when I was getting used to the pigeons!"

The bag was whisked into a lead box and the lid was locked down tight. The box was then placed inside another lead box inside a steel-clad compartment inside the van. The bomb-proof doors were slammed shut and the van zoomed away, siren screaming: EEE-AHH ... EEE-AHH ... EEE-AHH!

"Oh, this is exciting," said Mr Biz. "Although it could be a trifle less dark, one supposes."

"I wonder what they're going to do with us?" Bunny said.

"Don't you know?" growled the sour bear.

"If I knew," Bunny informed him, "I shouldn't wonder."

"Well, before I bite your nose off, I'll tell you. What's going to happen to us is what happens to all unexploded bombs in the city of London ..."

"I'm not sure I want to know," said the clown, trembling a little.

"They explode them, of course," finished Grizzle. "That's what they do: tie dynamite to the package and explode the whole thing!"

"Oh, dear! Oh, my! Oh, me!" shrieked Mr Biz. "I don't like the sound of that at all!"

"BLAMMO! KERPLOOEY!" rumbled the bear. "Fluff from one end of London to the other!"

"I think I'm going to faint!" cried Mr Biz.

"Grizzle, do you mind?" snapped Bunny. "We have enough to worry about without you scaring everyone. They're not going to explode us."

"Of course they are! BLAMMO! KER-PLOOEY!"

"No they're not. They'll look in the bag and see that we're not a bomb and they'll ... they'll ..."

"They'll what? Make us Lord Mayor of London? Not likely. I say they'll explode us."

So, there they were, riding in a lead box in the back of a Bomb Squad van on the way to be exploded into a very great quantity of singed fluff.

This, Bunny thought, had a way of making everything else that had happened so far appear uneventful, boring even.

If I ever live through this, old Bun promised himself, I will never complain about being lost again.

13

Being Exploded

The policemen drove the van to a deserted field where, as Grizzle suggested, they did indeed explode the bombs they collected. Carefully, the bomb disposal men slid the lead box from the van, and lifted the bag from the box with a very long pole.

"I'll get the dynamite," said one of the policemen.

"Righty-ho!" said the other. "I'll just carry this to the centre of the field."

"Did you hear that?" Mr Biz whispered sharply. "They're going to *explode* us!"

"I *told* you they would," replied Grizzle. He sounded really pleased to have finally said something important.

"Do something!" cried Mr Biz. "I'm allergic to fluff."

"Ross would know what to do," said Bunny. "He was always a good one in a tight spot. That boy had a brain in his bonnet."

"Fat lot of good that does us now," muttered the bear. "He might be Super Gran herself for all it matters to us."

"Oh, my! Oh, me!" sighed the gloomy clown. "To end up like this. If Hamley's could see me now. Dear, dear!"

"Shh!" shushed Bunny. "Let me think."

He thought and he thought, and what he thought was, "I'd better think of something quick — or BLAMMO! KERPLOOEY! We're fluff!"

"Hold on, what's this?" He looked down and saw that one of his dangly legs was hanging out of the bag through a hole which the pigeons had pecked in the plastic.

"That's it!" he thought. "If I can make the hole a little larger, maybe we can slip through."

And he started pushing with all his might. The plastic stretched and stretched, and he succeeded in getting his other leg out and there he stuck.

Just then the plastic bag lightly touched ground. A voice floated down from somewhere above them. "Here's the dynamite," the voice said.

"Well, that's it," muttered Grizzle.

Mr Biz started to cry.

Bunny tried to wriggle, but the bag was on the ground and his legs were hanging out and he couldn't budge a bit.

There was a rustle above them as the policeman picked up the bag and put the dynamite beneath it. "It's now or never!" cried Bunny. With all his strength he pushed and pushed again...

Now, just at this point, it might be pleasant to report that he wriggled his way out of the bag and saved the day with an astonishing display of heroics. But, unfortunately, that is not what happened. What did happen was this: Bunny pushed and his legs slipped out a little further. Not much. Not enough to wriggle out. But enough to be noticed, because the next thing the three in the bag heard was:

"What's all this then?"

And:

"I say, the bag's got legs! Brown fuzzy legs."

Then, very, very carefully the bag opened and two policeman-type faces peered in.

"It's just a load of stuffed toys!" the policemen said together.

The policemen were very relieved not to have a bomb on their hands. They took off their padded gloves and helmets and sat back on their heels. "Well, this is one for the books," they said.

Then they gathered up their equipment and tossed the bag of toys back into the van and returned to police headquarters. There the bag was tagged and carried downstairs to a room that looked like an enormous steel cage full of shelves.

On each shelf was a cubby-hole, and in each cubby-hole was a tagged something: a lady's purse containing six pounds, forty-eight pence and an Underground ticket; a cricket bat; a gold watch with a cracked glass; a pair of black leather gloves and a length of pipe which had been used in a break-in; a red transistor radio; two Rolls Royce tyres; a barrister's white wig; an electric guitar with four strings ... and ... well, one gets the idea: a very great lot of odds and ends of things that had only one thing in common: they were OFFICIAL POLICE PROPERTY.

14

In the Slammer

The toys were taken by a nice policewoman in a blue uniform and placed on one of the shelves with the plastic Sainsbury's bag. This was usual in cases like this. OFFICIAL POLICE PROPERTY was kept in the steel cage in case it was needed as evidence of a crime or someone came to claim it, which was rare indeed.

The policewoman wrote on the tag:

Number: 59088-444
Item(s): Stuffed toys (3)
Disposition: Unknown
Officer: RLT

She hung the tag on the peg over the cubbyhole and then closed the cage, turned out the lights, and went to have her tea.

"Ooo, it's dark in here," complained Mr Biz.

"And chilly. I don't think I'm going to like this at all."

Bunny was about to point out that it could be worse, and that, just for instance, it was a whole lot better than being blown to smoking fluff with dynamite.

He was about to say this, but he didn't get the chance because a deep, rusty-sounding voice interrupted him. "What are you going to do about it, huh?" the voice said. "Ha! You mamma's boys are all alike. You make me sick, the lot of you!"

"Who said that?" growled Grizzle. "Come over here and I'll bite your nose off!"

"Yeah? I'd like to see you try," replied the voice. "I don't think you're brave enough."

"Oh, yeah?" said the grumpy bear.

"Yeah!" said the voice.

"Oh, yeah?" said Grizzle.

This might have gone on quite a long time, so Bunny shouted: "Please! Will everyone just be quiet?" That got their attention, so he said, "Thank you. Now then, who is speaking to us?"

"Me. I am."

"Please, who is 'Me' and where are you?"

From out of the shadows of a cubby-hole on the shelf directly opposite them waddled a

lumpish, squat figure of a bulldog. This bulldog
had a straw hat and a cigar, both of which were
real although he himself was made of white
towelling.

"Oh, there you are," said Bunny. "My name is
Bunny Rabbit, and these are my friends, Grizzle
Bear, and Mr Biz."

"Humph!" snorted the bulldog. "A bunch of
toys!"

"Look who's talking!" growled Grizzle.
"Come over here, and I'll bi ..."

"That's enough, Grizzle," said Bunny. "I don't
believe I caught your name," he told the dog.

"I never threw it! Arf, arf, arf," the dog
chuckled.

"Very amusing," replied Bunny. "I must
remember that."

"My name is Jack," said the bulldog. "What
are you in for?"

"Sorry?"

"How come they threw you in the slammer?"

"The slammer?" wondered Bunny.

"The joint, the big house, the block, Her
Majesty's B & B – this place here? What crime
did you commit?"

"We didn't do anything," offered Mr Biz. "It
was all a dreadful mistake. We're innocent."

"That's what they *all* say," puffed the dog.

"Well, now that you mention it," replied Bunny, "we *were* sort of impersonating a bomb."

"Oh, terrorists," sneered Bulldog Jack. "You're the worst."

"No, no," said Bunny quickly, "we weren't actually a bomb. Someone just thought we were and ... Well, to cut a long story short: here we are."

"And here you'll stay, too," Jack told them. "Nobody, but nobody, gets out of the slammer. Ever."

"Ever?"

"Never!" grunted Jack. "Look at me — I've been in here twenty-two years so far."

"What are you in for?" asked Grizzle.

"Oh, some dimwit threw me through a glass shop window on election night, and I was confiscated by the cops as evidence."

"And you're still here?" marvelled Bunny.

(I should like to interrupt here to point out that Jack was a little out in his calculations. He had not, in fact, been in the slammer twenty-two years. He had been there a little less than five. It is a small matter, I know, but it may be important later on.)

"I hope *we* won't be here that long," sighed Mr Biz.

"You got any friends on the outside, Clown?"

asked Jack.

"Well, there's Trixie," said Mr Biz. "But she's not much of a friend really. More like a disease, if you must know."

"This Trixie dame know you're in here?"

"No, I suppose not."

"Then you're in for a l-o n-g stretch, believe me. The l-o-n-g-e-s-t. They'll be sending rockets to Mars before *you* three get out."

"They already are," said Bunny.

"You don't say," mused Bulldog Jack. "Like I said, I've been in here a long time. And so will you, so you'd better get used to it."

15

Getting Used to it – Sort of

What Bulldog Jack had said was true. Since no one really knew that the stuffed toys were in the slammer, no one could be expected to come and bail them out. Their only hope was that the Queen would declare an amnesty and set all the prisoners free – something which had not happened since Alfred the Great, I believe.

Day in, day out they waited. Week in, week out. One month went by. And then another, and another. And, contrary to what Bulldog Jack had said, they *didn't* get used to it. What is more, the longer they waited, the more they felt as if they *never would* get used to it.

Days, weeks, months passed and they waited for something to happen.

Nothing happened. No one came.

No one, that is, except the nice policewoman

who sometimes appeared with an umbrella which had been used in a robbery, or a coil of rope found in mysterious circumstances. She always smiled when she saw the stuffed toys, but she went about her business just the same. So it looked as if our friends were in for a rather long stretch. Indeed, they might still have been there at this very moment – and this would have been the end of our story (and a pretty sorry end, too) – if it hadn't been for the very simple fact of Christmas.

What does Christmas have to do with it, you might ask?

I'll tell you. It seems that there is an obscure law on the books which says that once every five years all the various items of OFFICIAL POLICE PROPERTY which have not been claimed, and which are not material evidence in court cases currently before the bar, and which are not required for "helping police with their inquiries", may be disposed of in any reasonable manner.

One morning our friends woke up to a clatter of steel bars, and a dozen removal men wearing blue overalls marched in and began throwing things into boxes. The nice policewoman stood by with a clip-board full of papers and checked the items off the list.

By two o'clock that afternoon it was over. Every shelf and cubby-hole was empty and swept clean — except one.

"That's the lot, miss," said the head removal man. "There's just those stuffed toys left." He jerked a thumb at Grizzle, Bunny, and Mr Biz, who quivered just a little.

"We've run out of boxes just now. I'll 'ave me mate clear 'em out as soon as 'e gets back."

The nice policewoman looked right at Bunny and bit her lip as if she were trying very hard to think of something.

"Oh..." she said, "don't bother."

"Won't be no bother, miss. Then we'll be all square."

But the policewoman had made up her mind. "That won't be necessary. *I'll* take care of them myself. I know just the place for them." With that she scooped them up and tucked them under her arm.

"I suppose you had better take this one too, then," the removal man said. He reached into a box and pulled out Bulldog Jack. She carried them all upstairs where they were propped on a chair behind the door of the nice policewoman's office.

It was there that Bunny saw the calendar hanging on the wall above them. "Look," he said to the others. "It's December already. December the fifteenth. Christmas will be here before we know it."

"Christmas in a police station," sighed Mr Biz sadly. "Not my idea of a fun time."

"Get used to it," growled Bulldog Jack. "We'll never get out of here – Christmas or not."

"I don't like Christmas anyway," grumbled Grizzle. He was lying, but no one said anything about it because they were all feeling a little sad just at that moment.

And I think I'm feeling a little sad, too, now that I mention it.

16

Nothing to Sneeze at

The toys really had no reason to think that anything good was about to happen to them. What with all they'd been through, it seemed that things only went from bad to worse and never got any better in between.

Life is like that. And then, suddenly, just when it appears that nothing good will ever happen again... PRESTO! Something good happens. That's Providence in operation, of course. Toiling away, sight unseen, bending all ends to the good.

Anyway, our friends had forgotten all about this. What with one thing and another. But the nice policewoman had had an idea down there in the slammer. And she had not forgotten it.

So, on the sixteenth of December, a Friday, when she went to turn off her office lights and go home for the weekend, she gathered up the box behind the door and put it in the boot of her car.

The next day she drove to her mum's house out in the country somewhere near Surrey, and gave the box to her. "Here are the toys I told you about, Mum," she said. "I do hope I'm not too late."

The next thing the toys saw was a round smiling face peering down at them and exclaiming, "Why, they'll do just the trick, they will. Thank you, Rita, dear. They'll be lovely. The ladies will be so pleased and, dear, you're just in time."

Then Rita's mother carried the box into her flat and announced to a whole room full of little old ladies, "More toys!"

The toys were placed on top of a very large pile of cotton wool. They looked around and saw five or six tables with sewing-machines, and scissors, and scraps of cloth, and bits of yarn and thread and needles all over them. And at each table a little old lady had a stuffed toy — or pieces of a stuffed toy — upon which she was sewing.

"Oh, no!" cried Mr Biz. "They're chopping us to pieces!"

"Just as I thought," growled Bulldog Jack. "It's one of those chop-shops you hear so much about. They chop you up for scrap and sell the

pieces on the black market."

"Let them try that with me," muttered Grizzle, "and they'll lose their noses!"

"Oh, that one just cut the head off the little teddy bear!" shrieked the clown. "It's terrible! I can't watch!"

"No, look!" said Bunny. "They're not chopping them apart, they're patching them up and putting them back together!"

It was true. Thanks to Providence, the toys had not fallen in with a gang of cut-throat grannies, but with a Ladies' Aid Society. This Ladies' Aid Society's special interest was in mending toys for needy children.

"Don't you see?" cried Bunny with relief. "We're saved!" And they were.

Over the course of the next few hours, Grizzle's missing ear was replaced and he was fitted with a new glass eye. Mr Biz had the sour frown washed off his face and a bright new smile painted on. Bulldog Jack had his mouldy cigar removed and his dingy white terrycloth was shampooed and brushed until it positively gleamed. Bunny had his head and arms and legs sewed on more tightly, and his blue bloomers were washed and mended and the buttons replaced.

And when all three were cleaned and brushed

and spiffed up smart, they looked just like new. Then Rita's mum put a big red ribbon around Grizzle, who grunted mildly but for once didn't mention biting anyone's nose off. Mr Biz was given a bright green bow to wear. And then he and Grizzle and Bulldog Jack were popped into a box with a lot of other stuffed toys to be sent to the Salvation Army to be given away.

But when Bunny's turn came . . .

Well, Rita's mum picked up Bunny and studied him hard for a minute and said, "Hold on, I know just the thing for you." And she put him in another box, and set him aside.

"Goodbye, Bunny!" called Mr Biz, smiling. "It's been good to know you."

"Goodbye, Mr Biz! Goodbye, Grizzle! Goodbye to you, too, Bulldog Jack! Have a Happy Christmas everyone!"

Yes, Christmas. I had almost forgotten about that. Christmas was only eight days away. Keep that in your head if you can.

17

A Slight, but Necessary, Digression

Now, just at this moment we must bring to mind a fairly grim fact of life — that Christmas cannot always be happy, or merry, or glad, or even bearable for some unfortunate people.

Sick people, poor people, worried people all have a miserable time at Christmas, and this is why we must remember them, and help them however we can. Christmas is a perfect time for remembering, helping, and sharing.

For example, I don't know if you know anything about hospitals but they are not the sort of places you'd want to spend a long time in — all those white walls and dreary corridors, and beds filled with miserable people. It's not the place to spend more than an afternoon, let alone a joyous holiday like Christmas — if you have the choice.

Unfortunately, not everyone has the choice, and that's that.

So, here we are, stuck in a hospital bed smelling those hospital smells, eating that hospital food, and wishing, hoping, praying to get well so we can get out in time to enjoy Christmas. Or, if not, that we might find a friend to make the long, lonely days a little easier to bear.

That's how it is for some people at Christmas. I just thought you should know about this because it may come in a bit later.

18

A Race Against Time

Rita's mum took the box Bunny was in and wrapped it up in red-and-green tissue paper, covered that with plain brown paper and carried it down to the local Post Office.

After waiting in the queue for nearly fifteen minutes — oh, the Post Office is a busy place this time of year! — the man behind the desk weighed the package and gave Rita's mum some stamps. She stuck them on and slid the package back across the counter to him.

"I can't promise this will get there in time for Christmas," he warned. "It's a fair journey — that long way to Scotland."

"Do your best, love," smiled Rita's mum. "That's all you can do, isn't it."

The postman looked at the address on the package:

Head Nurse
St Andrews Hospital
St Andrews
Kingdom of Fife
Scotland

Then he reached for a special stamp that read:
PRIORITY MAIL. He stamped the package
once, then once again, and tossed it into a
canvas bin marked SPECIAL HANDLING. He
smiled at Rita's mum and called, "Merry Christmas! Next, please!"

"At last," thought Bunny. "I'm finally on my
way home to Ross — I hope."

Now it was a race against time.

The gears of the Post Office grind slowly,
they say, but they grind exceedingly fine — or
something like that. I won't go into it all, but
once Bunny was inside the postal system I don't
think even Queen Elizabeth Her Royal Self could
have helped in any way.

What with laws, and acts, and Official Reg-
ulations, systems within systems, wheels within
wheels, and long-established Ways of Doing
Things, there was nothing anyone could do but
wait: wait for the sorters, the handlers, the sifters
and carriers, and the bins, vans, lorries, trains,
and bicycles . . . wait for them all to do their jobs

and whittle away at the absolute mountains of mail that must be moved before Christmas Day.

Well, the days crept by: December 22 ... 23 ... 24 ...

It was the morning of Christmas Eve, and there was Bunny on a train somewhere between Carlisle and Dundee, and it was snowing. Things were slowing down. Creeping along, actually.

In this race against time, Bunny was losing. It would have taken an Act of Parliament to get things speeded up even a little. But Parliament, like everyone else, was on its way home for Christmas.

Everyone else, that is, except Bunny ... and a little boy in Room 206 at St Andrews Hospital in the ancient and honourable Kingdom of Fife. The little boy in Room 206 was seven or eight years old and, truth to tell, he had not been feeling well for many, many long, dreary months. What was wrong with him, we don't rightly know, but it was something serious. Consequently, he had not set foot outside the hospital in a very long while. And his mother, God bless her, was very anxious and worried about him, as any mother would be.

To make matters worse, it was clear that the little boy would *not* be going home for Christmas. In fact, it appeared that there would *be* no

Christmas for him. His mum had spent nearly all her money on trying to help her little boy to get well and, to put it bluntly, there was simply no money for presents this year. And maybe not for a long, long time to come.

It was very sad, but that was that.

19

A Little Christmas Magic

There is something special about Christmas — that one day among all the others when people everywhere celebrate the birthday of Jesus. Christmas is magic. And it is that spark of Christmas magic that makes grown-ups behave as if they're children and makes children absolutely giddy.

This special magic is very potent stuff. It can make gruff people smile and grumpy people laugh; old people feel a little younger, and everyone — young and old alike — has a special sparkle in their eyes and a carol in their hearts.

And because of this magic, ordinary people will do extraordinary things: a butcher will trim off the extra fat from a chop; a shop assistant will greet a customer with a smile and a "Merry Christmas, how may I help you?"; and a postman will stay on and deliver that one, last, least, extra package.

If you are wondering where this magic comes from, I'll tell you. God put it there. It's as simple as that. So it won't surprise you terribly, I suppose, when I tell you that a foot-weary postman arrived at St Andrews Hospital on his way home from an exhausting long day delivering Christmas post. It was long past dark and he was tired, but something inside him made him want to deliver this last package before going home to his own Christmas.

"Merry Christmas!" he called cheerily, as he handed the package to the head nurse. "The last of the day — and I'm home for my haggis! Cheers!" The Head Nurse opened the package and read the note enclosed:

Here is a special gift for a special person. I don't know who it might be, but I think you'll know. Merry Christmas.

Your Cousin, Wanda.

The Head Nurse took one look at the red-and-green tissue-wrapped package and said to herself, "Indeed I do! I know just the place for this."

And she took the package directly to Room

206. Room 206 is where the little sick boy lay in bed facing a perfectly wretched Christmas. A little sick boy who, by the most remarkable of coincidences, was also named Ross: Ross McArthur McNelson McGregor McTavish Dundee, to be precise. McRoss, they called him for short.

McRoss lay listlessly on his pillow, his face turned to the window, gazing out on the lights of the city, wishing he could go home — knowing he couldn't — and hoping for a present that he knew he would not get. In short, feeling just about as miserable as it is possible for a little boy to feel.

McRoss's mother had just arrived and was taking off her coat, preparing to spend Christmas Eve by his bedside, and to cheer him up if she could.

She heard a "Psst" from the hall and saw the Head Nurse with a brightly-wrapped package in her hands.

She stepped into the hall, a question on her lips, and the Head Nurse said, "This just came for the laddie."

The laddie's mother looked at the package and said, "But there must be some mistake. I don't know who would send..."

"No mistake," said the Head Nurse with a

smile, and pressed the gift into her hands. "I'm very certain."

The mother accepted the package and carried it to the bed where she placed it on the covers under the little boy's chin.

"Look, love," she said, "someone has sent you a Christmas present."

The little boy's head spun around. "Have they?"

Then he saw the red-and-green package on the covers. "Oh, they have! What can it be?"

"Open it and find out," his mother said — which is what grown-ups always say at times like this.

He picked up the box carefully, shook it — it bumped a little, but did not rattle — peeled away the paper from one corner, and peered into the box. He saw two long brown ears.

Instantly, his little fingers were tearing the wrapping. Another instant and he was opening the box. And a split-second later he was crushing Bunny to his chest in what was perhaps the biggest hug possible for anyone of his age to give.

"A bunny!" he cried, all excited. "Mother, this is the best Christmas present ever!"

"Oh, isn't he handsome!" exclaimed his mother, looking at Bunny's soft brown fur and

his spiffy blue bloomers. "He is a fine friend, indeed. Whatever will you call him?"

"I'll call him . . . " McRoss thought for a moment. "Brown-Ears!" he cried, "because that's the first thing I saw of him."

"A fine name," his mother said.

All this time, Bunny was thinking. "This little boy is very like Ross," he thought. "He even has the same name — sort of. I am sure he'll make a good master . . . Oh, but I miss Ross so much — especially now. At Christmas."

Bunny was feeling a little sad at this moment, but then he heard the boy say, "I prayed for a present, mother. I prayed so hard. I prayed that God would send me something and he did! Brown-Ears is going to be my very good friend."

"That's right," said his mother. "Now, you must take a little nap. I will be here when you wake up and we can talk and have a Christmas sweetie."

Little McRoss pulled Bunny up close to his cheek and hugged him tight, closed his eyes and went to sleep.

His mother sat beside the bed, watching silently. Suddenly Bunny heard a soft sound. He looked up. The mother had tears in her eyes and was sniffling a little, and smiling.

She put a hand on Bunny's head and whispered, "I don't know where you have come from, Rabbit. But you are indeed the answer to a little boy's prayers — and to his mother's."

Well, later that night when his new master was sound asleep, Bunny closed his eyes and prayed that somehow God would help his dear old friend Ross to understand that his new friend needed him very, very much. Perhaps even more than his old master did.

And even though he would still miss Ross, and think about him from time to time, remembering the good times they had had growing up together, good friend that he was, Bunny would stay where he was needed most.

"Because," he thought to himself, "that's how it is when you are the answer to someone else's prayers."